To Tor, for the inspiration to write this story, and to all the Papa Pufferbellies cheering on their children. — S.S.

• Library of Congress Cataloging-in-Publication Data • Names: Shaskan, Stephen, author, illustrator. • Title: Big Choo / by Stephen Shaskan. • Description: New York : Scholastic Press, an imprint of Scholastic Inc., [2018] • Summary: Little Choo wants to be just like his father Papa Pufferbelly, but pulling a line of freight cars up a steep mountain might be a little too much for the small engine. Identifiers: LCCN 2017004711 | ISBN 9780545708579 • Subjects: LCSH: Railroad trains—Juvenile fiction. | Locomotives—Juvenile fiction. Perseverance (Ethics)—Juvenile fiction. • Confidence—Juvenile fiction • CYAC: Railroad trains—Fiction. • Size—Fiction. • Perseverance (Ethics)—Fiction. • Fathers and sons—Fiction. • Classification: LCC PZ7.S532418 Bi 2018 • DDC [E]—dc23 • LC record available at https://lccn.loc.gov/2017004711 • ISBN 978-0-545-70857-9 • 10 9 8 7 6 5 4 3 2 1   18 19 20 21 22 • Printed in China 38

First edition, March 2018 • Book design by Doan Buu

BIG CHOO

STORY AND PICTURES
BY
STEPHEN SHASKAN

SCHOLASTIC PRESS • NEW YORK

Early in the morning, Little Choo and Papa Pufferbelly
rolled down by the station. Little Choo's boiler bubbled.
It was going to be a big day!

Little Choo always wanted to be just like his Papa —
brave, fast, and strong.
"Papa, Papa! I'm ready to ride the main line today!"
"Are you sure, Little Choo?" asked Papa.

Little Choo puffed up his chest;
he knew the main line wasn't for little trains.

"I'm not Little Choo!" he said.
"I'm BIG CHOO! Just like you, Papa!"

"Okay, Big Choo, full steam ahead!" said Papa.

CLICKETY-CLACK!

For the first time, Big Choo rolled off the
little loop and switched onto the main line.

"I'm brave, Papa! Watch me roll over this old bridge all by myself!"
And even though the river rushed below, Big Choo kept his pilot straight
and pushed on.

CHUGGA-CHUGGA!
CHUGGA-CHUGGA!

And Papa Pufferbelly cheered,

CHOO! CHOO!

"I'm faster than a speeding bullet train, Papa!"
Big Choo primed his pistons. "Catch me if you can!"

CHUGGA-CHUGGA!
CHUGGA-CHUGGA!

And Papa Pufferbelly cheered,

CHOO! CHOO!

"I'm strong too, Papa!" said
Big Choo. "Even my tender is tough!
Watch me haul this freight!"

Big Choo cranked his engine
in reverse and coupled up to
a line of freight cars.

CLINK-CLANK!

CHUGGA-CHUGGA!
CHUGGA-CHUGGA!

And Papa Pufferbelly cheered,

CHOO! CHOO!

Big Choo was brave, fast, and strong, just like his papa!

His big day was chugging along without a hitch.

"I bet . . . I can haul all these freight cars up that humongous mountain."

"That's quite a load," said Papa. "Are you sure you're ready?"

"I'm sure, Papa. I'm BIG CHOO!"

Big Choo pushed his throttle forward and charged up the mountain as fast as he could go!

CHUGGA-CHUGGA!
CHUGGA-CHUGGA!

And Papa Pufferbelly cheered,

CHOO! CHOO!

Big Choo's wheels slipped!
He started sliding backward!
He lost control!
OH NO!

BIG CHOO DERAILED!

Papa Pufferbelly raced to his son.
"Are you okay, Big Choo?"

"Papa, I'm not Big Choo," sniffed the young train.
"I'm just Little Choo."

"You are brave, fast, strong, and smart!" said Papa.
"Don't let a little tumble ruin your big day."
FULL STEAM AHEAD!

Big Choo puffed up his chest.
"Maybe I just need to take my time."
"Let's get you back on track!" said Papa.

Big Choo headed back up
the mountain again.

CHUGGA-CHUGGA!
CHUGGA-CHUGGA!

And Papa Pufferbelly cheered,

CHOO! CHOO!

Big Choo's pumps puffed hard!

PUFF! PUFF! PUFF! PUFF!

His couplings cringed!

ERRRRRRRRR!

But his wheels held strong!

CHUGGA-CHUGGA! CHUGGA-CHUGGA!

And Papa Pufferbelly cheered,

CHOO! CHOO!

It was a big day for Big Choo.
He was brave, fast, strong, and smart, just like his papa!
"Now watch me go into that scary, dark tunnel!"

"Let's save that for another day," said Papa Pufferbelly.
And Big Choo and Papa Pufferbelly rolled back home.

"Good night, Papa!"
"Good night, Big Choo!"

A NOD TO VIRGINIA LEE BURTON

As a child, my father read to me *Mike Mulligan and the Steam Shovel* and *The Little House* by Virginia Lee Burton. I was always enamored by the art; so beautiful, sophisticated, and simply perfect. While creating the world of *Big Choo*, I drew a lot of inspiration from *The Little House* and had the pleasure of studying all the original paintings for *The Little House*, which are kept at the Kerlan Collection here at the University of Minnesota. I'm amazed by how Virginia Lee Burton formed a believable landscape out of simple abstract shapes; she created realistic worlds that are beyond reality. What appears to be naïve is the construction of complex two-dimensional dioramas that are pure genius. I am and will always be a humble fan.

— STEPHEN SHASKAN